Dunrea
rea, Olivier
eon /
99

Gideon

Olivier Dunrea

HOUGHTON MIFFLIN HARCOURT
Boston   New York

To access the read-along audio, visit
WWW.HMHBOOKS.COM/FREEDOWNLOADS
ACCESS CODE: PLAYTIME

AGES	GRADES	GUIDED READING LEVEL	READING RECOVERY LEVEL	LEXILE® LEVEL
4–6	1	E	7–8	260L

www.hmhco.com

The text of this book is set in MShannon.
The illustrations are pen and ink and gouache on140-pound d'Arches coldpress watercolor paper.

The Library of Congress Cataloging-in-Publication Data is on file.

ISBN: 978-0-544-43059-4 paperback
ISBN: 978-0-544-43058-7 paper over board

Manufactured in China
SCP 10 9 8 7 6 5 4 3 2

4500531051

For Ayden—welcome to the family!

This is Gideon.

Gideon is a small, ruddy
gosling who likes to play.
All day.

Gideon marches
to the piggery.

He plays chase-the-piglet.

Gideon dashes
to the henhouse.

He plays find-the-eggs.

"Gideon, time for your nap,"
his mother calls.

"No nap! I'm playing!"

Gideon hops to the field.

He plays tag-the-mole.

Gideon chases butterflies
in the meadow.

He sneaks behind a beetle
on a rock.

"Gideon, time for your nap,"
his mother calls.

"No nap! I'm playing!"

Gideon scurries to the pond.

He splashes
with the ducklings.

Gideon scoots to the beehives.

He listens to the bees
buzzing inside the hive.

"Gideon, time for your nap,"
his mother calls.

"No nap! I'm playing!"

Gideon scampers
to the sheep house.

He bounces on the back
of the ewe.

Gideon leaps
over a green frog.

He plays quietly
with a small turtle.

Gideon wanders to the field.

He scrambles to the top
of the haystack.

"Gideon, time for your nap,"
his mother calls.

Gideon doesn't answer.

Gideon is a small, ruddy
gosling who likes to play . . .
almost all day.
Shhh . . .